# Spike and Ali Enson

by Malaika Rose Stanley
Illustrated by Sarah Horne

Tamarind

SPIKE AND ALI ENSON
TAMARIND BOOKS 978 1 848 53023 2

Published in Great Britain by Tamarind Books,
a division of Random House Children's Books
A Random House Group Company

This edition published 2010

1 3 5 7 9 10 8 6 4 2

Text copyright © Malaika Rose Stanley, 2010
Illustrations copyright © Sarah Horne, 2010

The Random House Group Limited supports The Forest Stewardship Council
(FSC), the leading international forest certification organisation. All our titles
that are printed on Greenpeace approved FSC certified paper carry the FSC logo.
Our paper procurement policy can be found at www.rbooks.co.uk/environment

**Mixed Sources**
Product group from well-managed
forests and other controlled sources
www.fsc.org   Cert no. TT-COC-2139
© 1996 Forest Stewardship Council

TAMARIND BOOKS
61–63 Uxbridge Road, London, W5 5SA

www.tamarindbooks.co.uk
www.kidsatrandomhouse.co.uk
www.rbooks.co.uk

Addresses for companies within The Random House Group Limited
can be found at: www.randomhouse.co.uk/offices.htm
THE RANDOM HOUSE GROUP Limited Reg. No. 954009

A CIP catalogue record for this book is available
from the British Library.

Printed in the UK by CPI Bookmarque, Croydon, CR0 4TD

For Danjuma and Garikai
with love and thanks for
the inspiration

M.R.S.


For Sue, Gordon, Helen and Syd

S.H.

# Contents

# Chapter 1

## Over the Moon

Spike clamped his headphones over his ears and turned up the volume on his XP7 player. He closed his eyes and let his head flop forward until it was resting on the table. The heavy drum-beat pounded his brain until he thought his head would burst and splatter the whole kitchen, but he didn't care.

It was Friday afternoon. After a hard week at school, with Mr Ford and the

Lovelace Twins, anything was better than listening to his baby brother who was screaming in the front room.

Spike frowned. According to Dad, babies needed peace and quiet. That was why Spike's drum-kit had been moved out to the garden shed. But Ali Enson was always screaming his head off, light-years away from peace or quiet. His screams could reach a million decibels.

Spike listened to the music but after a while, he could hear a faint screeching sound as well as the thumping beat.

He took off the headphones and turned round towards the front room. Ali had finally stopped crying.

The screeching noise was Mum. "Spiiiiike!"

"What's the matter?" called Spike. "Is your back hurting again?"

He went into the front room and knelt down. Mum had pulled a muscle in her back a few days ago. Now she was under strict instructions from the doctor to lie flat on the floor.

She peered up at him and grinned. Her lipstick was smudged and her nail polish was chipped. There was a trickle of something yellow and yucky down the front of her tracksuit.

"My back's just the same," said Mum. "But now I have a sore throat as well. I have been calling you for ages."

"Sorry," said Spike.

"Listen, love," said Mum. "Ali needs some fresh air. Do you think you could take him out for a walk?"

Spike groaned.

"Come on," begged Mum. "With me out of action, your dad has been running around after Ali all day. He has just popped upstairs for a bit of a lie-down.

He really needs to have a rest."

"It's not fair," said Spike, glancing towards the carry-cot. "All any of us ever do is run around after Ali."

"Don't exaggerate," said Mum. "I have told you a zillion times. He's not that bad."

"He is!" cried Spike. "When's the last time Dad did any knitting or went to yoga? When's the last time you went skate-boarding or hang-gliding? I can't even remember the last time we did anything together!"

"How can I go hang-gliding when I have practically broken my back?" said Mum.

"Ali's fault!" said Spike triumphantly. "If you hadn't been lugging him up and down the stairs and round and round the garden, it would never have happened. He must weigh a tonne."

"Seven point two kilos," said Mum.

"I have been on this planet for years and years," said Spike. "I was happy. I liked being an only child. Ali's been here ten minutes and he has ruined my life!"

"Six months," said Mum. "He will be six months on Thursday. Now take him out, Spike. Please."

Spike pushed the buggy through the front door and gently bumped it down the step. But it wasn't gentle enough. Ali whimpered. Then he sucked in a huge lungful of air and began to howl at the top of his voice. Behind them, Mum called out last-minute instructions but Spike pretended not to hear her.

He steered the buggy past the dustbins towards the garden gate and looked up and down the street.

Larry Skinner, from next door, was lying in the road in front of his house, fixing his motorbike.

On the other side of the street, Mr Rivers, their neighbour and good friend, was sculpting chickens into his privet with an electric hedge-trimmer.

Spike crossed over. One wrong move from Mr Rivers and the whole buggy could be accidentally hacked to pieces.

"Hi, Mr Rivers," yelled Spike over

the sound of Ali and the electric hedge-trimmer.

Mr Rivers turned off the machine and carefully laid it down on his garden path. He pulled up the front of his checked work-shirt and wiped sweat from his head and neck.

"Blimey. Your Ali's got some lungs on him. Are you taking him out for a walk, then?"

"Yes," said Spike. "Mum and Dad have conked out. I thought I would give them a break."

Mr Rivers wasn't listening. He was crouched over the buggy, tickling Ali's chin. Ali dribbled something green and slimy on to his fingers but Mr Rivers didn't even notice.

"Funny, isn't it?" he said, glancing up at Spike. "You look nothing like your dad but this little blighter is the spitting image of him."

It's not funny, thought Spike. It's just what happens when people adopt a kid because they can't make babies. Then years later they produce one of their own, thanks to the miracle of modern science. But Spike didn't say any of this out loud. He didn't think Mr Rivers would understand.

"Would you like to have him?" he said instead.

Mr Rivers straightened up quickly and pushed his shirt sleeves a bit further up his bulging, hairy, tattooed arms.

"Is that a joke?"

No, thought Spike. I'm deadly serious. If you want him, take him. He's free, no charge.

"Because it's not funny," said Mr Rivers. "If anything happened to Ali, it would break your mum and dad's hearts."

Well, that's where you are totally wrong, thought Spike. Mum's flat on her back with a pulled muscle and Dad's flat on his face with exhaustion. If something happened to Ali Enson, we would all be over the moon!

# Chapter 2

## Twin Terror

It was already late afternoon but this was the first warm day for ages. The park was packed. There were buggies and babies everywhere.

Spike tried to remember if it had always been like this. Perhaps he had just never noticed before he had a buggy and a baby of his own. He felt a stab of anger. Most of the babies were being looked after by their parents instead of their older brothers or sisters.

In fact, most of the older kids he could see were playing football or basketball.

Spike recognized Amarjit Singh from Year 8, doing his usual Premiership-striker impression.

A few kids, mainly girls, were charging around the adventure playground, playing a chasing game.

Spike strolled over to a bench and parked the buggy next to a litter bin. Ali had finally turned down the volume and decided to give his vocal chords a rest. His eyelids gradually closed against the glare of the setting sun.

After a while, when he was sure Ali was sleeping, Spike stood up and ambled over to the monkey bars. He grabbed the first rung and managed three or four hand-overs before he crashed to the ground in an untidy heap.

He glanced around, hoping no one had noticed. Then his heart stopped beating! The buggy was gone! Ali was gone!

Spike sped back to the bench and leaped on top of it, desperately craning his neck in all directions. Someone had kidnapped Ali! Someone had taken him away! For months, he had been hoping and wishing that Ali would disappear. But not like this! Mum would kill him!

"Oy! Enson!" shouted a voice from behind him.

Spike twisted round, lost his balance, toppled off the bench and practically fell into Ebony Lovelace's arms. He caught a quick glimpse of Kiera, her twin sister, holding Ali above her head and spinning away from the tangle of arms and legs.

Spike heard himself swear.

Somehow, he and Ali had both fallen into the terrifying grip of a Lovelace!

"Get off me!" snarled Ebony, shoving him away. "What are you doing?"

Spike stumbled, ducked under what might have been an incoming fist and lunged towards Kiera.

"What am *I* doing?" he yelled. "What are *you* doing? You can't just go around nicking other people's babies!"

He just managed to stop himself snatching Ali out of Kiera's arms. If it came to a fight, he knew he would lose. It would be two against one and both girls were huge and as hard as nails. He didn't fancy Ali's chances either. He would probably land on the ground and crack his head.

Spike held out his arms hoping that Kiera would understand and give back the baby.

"We weren't nicking him," she said,

glaring at Spike but gently rocking Ali from side to side. "We were looking after him."

"Yeah," agreed Ebony. "You abandoned him. You were neglecting him. We should phone Child Line. We should report you to Social Services."

"Right," said Kiera. "And I bet your mum would love to hear all about how you were playing on the monkey bars and left your little sister all on her own."

Ali gurgled happily, leaving no doubt about whose side he was on.

Spike had heard enough. "Brother!" he snapped. "He's a boy! Now give him back or I'll call the police."

Kiera scowled, but her expression melted as she looked down at Ali and carefully settled him back into the buggy.

Both girls folded their arms and

flicked their heads at the same time in that weird twin way. Any closer and they would have taken his eye out, thought Spike.

He peered down into the buggy. Ali was blowing bubbles, trying to look cute. To make matters worse, it seemed to be working.

"Aaaah," sighed Kiera. "He's gorgeous. What's his name?"

"Ali," said Spike. He grabbed the buggy and began to wheel it away. "What's it to you?"

"Don't be like that," said Kiera. "We like babies, don't we, Eb?"

"Yes, we do," said Ebony, stepping into his path. Her voice softened slightly but she still had her arms folded. "Tell your mum and dad, if they ever need a reliable baby-sitting service, they should call us."

"Our rates are very reasonable," added Kiera. "It's buy one, get one free."

Spike shuddered and tried to steer the buggy round Ebony. The last thing he wanted was the Lovelace Twins in his house, ooh-ing and aah-ing over Ali.

"Why don't you go and play football or something?" said Ebony, stepping into his way again. "Or have another go on the monkey-bars. We can look after Ali for a bit."

"I can't," said Spike. "My mum will be worried." He knew he was doing nothing for his already-battered reputation. "I have to go."

"Shall we walk you home then?" said Kiera. "We can make sure you are safe."

"I'm fine," said Spike. "I don't need body guards. I don't need baby-sitters."

The girls ignored him and fell into step on either side of him.

"He really is cute," said Kiera. "You should put him in for that Bonny Baby Competition down at the shopping centre."

"Bonny baby?" sneered Spike. "Give me a break! Anyway, my mum and dad aren't into competitions. They don't like losers. They prefer co-operation."

"Shame," said Ebony, frowning. "He

would win, no problem. First prize is a hundred pounds."

Tempting, thought Spike. But there was no way he was mentioning any part of this encounter with the Lovelace Twins to Mum, Dad or anyone else in the entire universe.

# Chapter 3

## Space Invaders

As soon as Spike reached home, Dad flew into the hallway and scooped Ali up into his arms.

"Hello, little man," he said.

He held Ali up and sniffed his bottom. Even through several layers of clothing, the smell was gut-wrenching and unmistakeable. Spike wished the Lovelace Twins had caught a whiff of it.

"New nappy for you, I think," said Dad, racing up the stairs. "Put the buggy away, son," he called back over his shoulder.

Spike sighed. He folded down the buggy and heaved it into the cupboard under the stairs.

He wandered back into the living room.

"Oh, Spike," said Mum. "Thanks for that, honey. That little break has done me and your dad the power of good. How was it? Did you have a nice time?"

Fantastic, thought Spike, if being mugged by the Lovelace Twins counts as nice.

"It was OK," he said gloomily.

"What's up?" said Mum. "Did something happen?"

"Nothing I want to talk about," said Spike. "Everything's under control." He wasn't sure if he was trying to convince himself or Mum.

"Are you sure?" said Mum.

"Yes," said Spike. He tried to change the subject. "I'm just a bit fed-up. I had a lunchtime detention today because Mr Ford thought I was talking in assembly when I wasn't."

"Are you sure?" said Mum.

"Why do you keep asking me that?" said Spike. "I should know if I was talking or not."

"OK," said Mum. "Take it easy. I believe you. But you aren't in assembly now. You are at home and it's the weekend. Why are you still in such a bad mood?"

Spike flopped onto the sofa. Mum just didn't get it.

"What difference does it make?" he said. "At school, Mr Ford and the Lovelace Twins make my life a misery. As soon as I get home, Ali takes over the job."

"Oh, Spike," laughed Mum. "You always exaggerate. Teachers sometimes make mistakes. I'm sure the Lovelace Twins are really nice boys and Ali's just a baby."

"Mum," said Spike. "You just don't understand."

After dinner, Spike escaped upstairs to his room. He played *21st Century Space Invaders* on his games console with his headphones on. He would rather have played his drums but it was too cold in the shed and there wasn't really enough elbow room.

Spike zapped a trio of laser-armed aliens and something poked him in the back. He leaped out of his chair and screamed. It was Dad.

"Are you trying to kill me?" Spike shouted. "I nearly had a heart attack! Don't creep up on people like that!"

"Sorry," mouthed Dad.

He reached out and took the headphones off Spike's ears.

"It's not really my fault, though. It's these wretched things," he said, waggling them up and down. "I knocked at the door. I shouted, but you were miles away."

Dad nodded in the direction of the screen. "Presumably on Planet What's-it."

"Planet OsKarbi," said Spike.

"Right," said Dad. He plonked himself on the bed and looked serious. "I have been talking to your mother. She thinks you are being picked on at school and neglected at home. She thinks you are suffering from a bit of sibling jealousy."

"What do you think?" said Spike.

"I think everything is probably hunky-dory," said Dad. He frowned.

"Except for the usual suspects for a lad your age. Mates. Girls. Teachers. Bullies."

Spike laughed. "Spot on," he said.

"Great," said Dad. He punched Spike's arm playfully and stood up to leave. "Goodnight, son."

"Dad, do you want to do something together tomorrow?" said Spike. "Swimming or bowling or something?"

"Sorry, son," said Dad. "You are on your own. We will do something as soon as your mother is back on her feet. Maybe next weekend. OK?"

"OK," said Spike.

He put his headphones back on and turned back to the screen. His life force had drained away. He was dead. He would have to start a new game.

Later, Spike lay in bed, tossing and turning, and thinking about how life had changed.

It hadn't always been like this. Before Ali was born, Mum and Dad had been the best parents in the world – probably the best in the universe!

To be fair, they weren't getting much sleep either. Spike could still hear Dad charging up and down the stairs, running around after Ali. A clean nappy... a bottle... another clean nappy and a complete change of clothes... two goes on the musical mobile followed by Dad's out-of-tune version of *Mirabelle McKenzie's Spaceship*... then back downstairs so Mum could feed Ali...

It was hard to believe that one tiny creature could cause so much trouble and produce such a huge quantity of vile-smelling waste products – and from both ends!

OK, for the last couple of weeks, Ali had been having the odd bowl of mashed carrot and sweet potato. But he was still mainly drinking Mum's breast milk. Spike had seen little bottles of the stuff in the fridge that she had squeezed out and saved.

He had even had a good sniff and dipped his finger in one to have a taste. It was thin and sweet like watered-down condensed milk. There was nothing to explain how Ali could have it inside his body for such a short time and change – no, transmute – it into such a vile, smelly, green substance.

Of course, the fact that Ali smelled like a baby-sized sewage works wasn't the only problem. He was weird in all sorts of ways. He could twist people round his little finger, not just Mum and Dad. Complete strangers fell in love with him.

He turned everyone into gibbering idiots. They ruffled his hair and chucked him under the chin and gurgled stupidly. They thought they saw a twinkle in his eyes instead of a suspicious glint. They thought he was exercising his lungs instead of torturing them and bursting their eardrums. They thought his skin was soft and brown and they never noticed the hint of scales or the greenish sheen.

Spike wasn't jealous. He just seemed to be the only one asking what Ali really was.

He suddenly sat bolt upright as the answer came to him in a flash. It was blindingly obvious. Ali Enson was an alien!

Mum had said for years that she could not have babies. So Ali must have been implanted into her belly by an extra-terrestrial from the Planet OsKarbi! She was in danger. They were all in danger... and it was up to Spike to save them!

# Chapter 4

## Alien Research

The next morning at breakfast, Spike could hardly keep his eyes open. He was so tired that he had to support his head with his hand to stop it crashing down into his cornflakes.

He had been awake half the night, trying to decide what to do about Ali.

"What did you decide?" said Dad.

Spike's head snapped up in alarm. "What?"

"What did you decide?" asked Dad.

"Swimming or bowling?"

Spike breathed a sigh of relief. "Neither," he said. "I'm not going."

"Come on, son," said Dad, looking guilty. "You know I can't leave Ali with your mother."

"It's OK," said Spike. "I have some research to do for... for a school project."

"Research?" said Dad. "Project?"

"Yes," said Spike, thinking fast. "Science and Technology. Where's the best place to find out about space travel and planets and stuff?"

"I'm not sure," said Dad. "What's wrong with the internet or the library?"

At the library, Spike watched as Larry Skinner dragged his fingers through his long greasy hair and slowly scratched his head.

Come on, thought Spike. I'm not asking you to fly me to Mars. You have had a whole term of the Young Librarian Training Scheme. You must have some idea where the books on space travel are kept.

"Why don't you have a look at the fantasy and science fiction comics?" said Larry. "We have loads of those."

"Larry," said Spike patiently. "I need facts, not fiction. Can't you look in the index on the computer?"

Larry's spotty face crumpled into a look of fear and confusion. "I haven't really got the hang of it yet. It's probably safer to wait until Mrs Thomas gets back."

Spike sighed. Why didn't Mrs Thomas sit next to the computer and eat a sandwich for lunch? Why did she have to disappear for a whole hour and leave Larry Skinner in charge?

"If you don't want to hang about," said Larry, "why don't you try the aquarium?"

"I think you mean the planetarium," said Spike. "But thanks, Larry. It's a great idea."

"Dad," said Spike, as he helped clear the table after lunch. "Can I have seven pounds?"

Dad dropped a plate. It crashed to the floor and shattered. Ali burst into tears and Mum started shouting from the front room.

"What's going on?" she yelled.

"Don't worry," called Dad. "Everything's under control." He looked at Spike. "What on earth do you need seven pounds for?"

"A pound for bus fares and six pounds to get in," said Spike.

Dad looked ready to ask another

question but Ali gave an ear-splitting scream and he changed his mind. He grabbed a teething ring from the table and pushed it into Ali's mouth. Then he grabbed a ten-pound note out of his wallet and pushed it into Spike's hand.

Spike stood beneath the domed roof of the planetarium and gazed up at the planets until he got a crick in his neck.

Earlier, he had noticed a sign that said guides were available to give further information and answer questions.

That's exactly what I need, thought Spike, as he went off in search of one. Someone who could guide Ali back to Planet OsKarbi or wherever it was he had come from.

"Excuse me," said Spike. "Where do you keep information on aliens?"

The guide had pinkish-blonde hair. She was wearing a navy-blue suit with a huge bow tied round the collar of her blouse. She looked him up and down and took a step backwards as if she was afraid he might try to undo her bow.

"The planetarium," she began, in a snooty voice, "is a scientific establishment dealing only with

astronomical facts. Aliens are fiction. They don't exist."

"How do you know?" asked Spike. "I thought scientists were supposed to keep an open mind."

"Mercury's too hot," explained the guide. "Jupiter and the outer planets are too cold. That leaves Venus and Mars. All the evidence indicates that they can't sustain life as we know it."

"What about life as we don't know it?" said Spike.

The guide closed her eyes and opened them again very slowly. "Even if other life-forms do exist, we will never find them and they will never find us."

"Why not?" asked Spike.

"Because the nearest star is Proxima Centauri and it would take seventy-five thousand years to get there!"

"Oh," said Spike gloomily.

The guide gave a smug smile. Then

she clutched her bow and leaned towards him. "If you are really interested in aliens, you might like to try the UFO Notification Centre. But be warned. The chap who runs that place is definitely off the planet!"

# Chapter 5

## First Contact

That evening, as usual, it took ages to put Ali to bed. Practically enough time to fly to Proxima Centauri and back, thought Spike, as he turned away from the sight of Dad changing Ali's fourth dirty nappy.

Mum had dozed off on the floor right after dinner but, amazingly, Dad was still going strong.

He was smiling and blowing raspberries on Ali's stomach and

saying, "What's up, little man? Aren't you tired yet?"

It was nine-thirty before Dad finally carried Ali upstairs and put him in the cot next to Mum's side of the bed.

Spike waited until Dad came back and settled down to watch the ten o'clock news. Then he went upstairs and listened at the door of Mum and Dad's bedroom. Ali was snoring.

Spike crept over to the bedside table and tapped in the number for the 24-hour hotline of the Unidentified Flying Object Notification Centre.

The phone was answered after just one ring and a man's voice with an American accent bellowed down the line.

"You fonk!"

"Sorry," whispered Spike. "I think I have the wrong number."

"You sure?" said the man. "This here's

the UFO Notification Centre. UFONC for short. Thomas J. Hoppermann speaking. TJ for short."

"Hello, TJ," whispered Spike. "Could you tell me if you are interested in aliens as well as UFOs?"

"Speak up!" bellowed TJ. "Can't hear you."

"Aliens," said Spike in a slightly louder whisper. "Are you interested in aliens?"

"You betcha!" said TJ. "You reckon you have seen one, kid?"

"Yes," said Spike, glancing over the edge of the cot at Ali. "He's right here."

"You sure? I wanna believe you, kid, but I have heard it all before. Folks stumbling around in the dark... some of them near-sighted, some of them blind drunk. Before you know it, they are calling all sorts of things aliens. Crash dummies, tree stumps, mail boxes, bull-frogs..."

"This one's a baby," said Spike.

"No kidding," said TJ. "How about that? A baby bull-frog."

Ali grunted in his sleep. Spike flinched and his voice came out in a strangled squeak. "No! A baby alien!"

"OK, take it easy," said TJ. "Don't want you scaring it away before we got the details down."

Spike peered down into the cot again. The beam of light from the landing didn't reach Ali's face, but even in the darkness Spike could see his eyes, now wide open and staring.

Oh no! That's all I need, thought Spike. If he starts crying, Dad will be up the stairs as fast as lightning.

But Ali didn't utter a sound. Even when Spike began answering TJ's long list of questions, Ali lay perfectly still and quiet. Watching. Listening.

"How big is it?" cried TJ.

"Small," whispered Spike. "Mum says he weighs about seven kilos."

"What colour?" said TJ.

"Dark brown on the outside," said Spike. "Green on the inside, judging by what comes out of him."

"No kidding," said TJ. "Has it tried to communicate?"

"He can't talk," said Spike. "He just screams and yells a lot. It seems to work though. Everyone does exactly what he wants."

"Sounds like quite a find," said TJ. "How about bringing it by the centre so I can examine it?"

"I don't think Dad will let me bring him across town on the bus," said Spike.

He paused. Ali had closed his eyes again. But now he was screwing up his face and his mouth was a gaping hole in the middle of it.

Spike recognized the signs. Any second now, Ali was going to start bawling.

"I have to go," whispered Spike.

"Gotcha," said TJ. "Here's what you need to do. Send me some

photographic evidence and a stool sample. That way I can run some tests."

"Send some what?" hissed Spike.

"Pictures and poop," said TJ. His voice was almost drowned out by Ali's first loud howl of protest. "Just put them in the post."

"Right," said Spike.

He slammed down the receiver and

darted across the landing to the safety of his own room. The door creaked noisily but he managed to click it shut just as Dad pounded up the last few stairs.

Spike leaned his back against the door. A wave of exhaustion washed over him and he slid onto the floor and hugged his knees. He sat there for a few minutes, listening to Ali's insistent, angry wail.

He knows I'm trying to get rid of him, thought Spike, feeling a flutter of fear in his stomach. Ali Enson knows.

# Chapter 6

## School Visit

The next day was Sunday and the post office was closed. In a way, Spike felt rather relieved. It gave him a whole day to think about two serious problems.

The first was how to send a sample of Ali's poo through the post. An envelope was out of the question. He would have to flatten the lumps and there was a risk that the squidgy bits would ooze out from under the flap.

The smell would be horrendous. Even a parcel would not hold that in!

The second problem was how to pinch a picture from Ali's *My First Year* book. It was in the cupboard in the front room. But with Mum lying on the floor, guarding it like a sentry, he probably would not be able to get near it for ages.

First thing Monday morning, Spike realized he had another, more pressing problem.

"You haven't forgotten Mr Ford's invitation, have you, love?" said Mum, when he went downstairs for breakfast.

"What invitation?" said Spike.

"Mr Ford asked me to bring Ali into school for his Personal, Social and Health Education lesson," said Mum. "Don't you remember?"

Suddenly Spike remembered. Of course he did! How could he have forgotten?

Spike had always suspected that Mr Ford hated children but since he had bumped into Mum and Ali in the supermarket, he had been really keen for them to come into school. It was like a nightmare version of Show and Tell!

"What a terrible shame you hurt your back," said Spike. "You won't be able to come now."

"Dad's bringing him instead," said Mum.

Spike's heart sank. Was there no escape from Ali?

"Eleven o'clock sharp," said Dad as he came in, cradling Ali in his arms.

"I think I will skip breakfast," said Spike. "I'm not hungry."

At school, nobody else in Spike's class remembered Ali's visit either. But Mr Ford soon reminded them.

"Right then, you lot. Shut up and listen. We will kick off with maths and then after break, we have PSHE. It will be a special lesson because Spike Enson's mother has agreed to bring in his baby brother for our Seven Ages of Man project."

Spike was sitting next to Ebony Lovelace and her hand shot up into the air with such speed and force, he was amazed she didn't dislocate her shoulder.

"Excuse me, Sir. Will that include women?"

"It doesn't have quite the same ring to it," said Mr Ford. "But yes, the Seven Ages of Man and Woman."

"My dad's coming instead, Sir," said Spike.

"All the better," said Mr Ford. "Perhaps that will satisfy Ebony Lovelace's demands for equal rights."

Spike watched as Ebony dug a hole into the desk with the point of her compass. He gave her a sympathetic nod but she scowled at him.

"Sexist pig," she muttered.

Spike hoped she meant Mr Ford and not him, but as he wasn't sure, he spent most of the maths lesson trying hard not to look at her.

At breaktime, Spike hid in the boys' toilets, although he wasn't sure he would be safe from the Lovelace Twins even in there.

When he dared to go back to the classroom, Dad was already sitting on Mr Ford's desk with Ali on his lap. Ali was gurgling and grinning. So was Mr Ford, which was pretty amazing because Spike had never even seen him smile before.

More amazing still, the entire class was gathered round Ali and everyone was pushing and shoving to get closer. The nearest kids were stroking his hair and holding his hands or tickling his chin. From what Spike could hear, they were all asking the usual, ridiculous baby questions.

"Isn't he beautiful?"

"You would never believe he was Spike Enson's brother, would you?"

"Coochie-coochie-coo. Who's a clever boy, then?"

"Hush now," said Mr Ford. "Let's find our seats and hear what Mr Enson has to tell us about babies."

Spike stopped listening as soon as Dad started going on about the miracle of childbirth and little bundles of joy. Instead, he found himself wondering how Ali had turned a bunch of hardened, street-wise kids – and the teacher from hell – into simpering idiots.

He looked around at their glazed, unblinking eyes. Every single one of them was fixed on Ali.

Ali was chewing Mr Ford's notes and dribbling on the register but no one else seemed to notice the sly smile that played across his lips or the wicked gleam in his eye.

Spike shivered. Didn't they see that Ali was tricking them? Using his alien powers to control them? He had to move fast. It wasn't just the safety of his own family that was at stake now. He had to save the whole universe!

# Chapter 7

## Photos and Poop

When the bell rang for lunch, Dad and Ali were swept into the playground by a crowd of demented baby-fans. Spike eyed them from the doorway. The whole thing was unbelievable. Tariq Jackson and Azif Hussein were practically drooling and he knew for a fact that they could not stand babies.

"Spike!" called Dad. "Why didn't you tell me that Kiera and Ebony had offered to baby-sit?"

"Yeah," growled Kiera. "Why didn't you tell him?"

"Sorry," said Spike as he shuffled towards them. "I forgot."

"I bet you didn't tell him about the Bonny Baby Competition they are running at the shopping centre either," snarled Ebony.

"Ha!" said Dad. "That bit doesn't surprise me. Competitions mean winners and losers. We aren't very keen on that sort of thing."

"You don't have to worry about losing," said Ebony. "Your Ali's bound to win. It's a guaranteed dead cert."

"Maybe," said Dad dreamily. He gazed at Ali and for a second, his eyes misted up. But he pulled himself together. "You are missing the point," he went on. "All babies are beautiful. How can anyone possibly choose a winner?"

"Easy," said Kiera. "They take loads

of pictures and then the judges decide."

Pictures? Spike almost felt his ears prick up and his eyes pop out.

"I told you, didn't I?" he said, looking straight at the twins and willing them to back him up. "*I* think it's a brilliant idea."

"Good grief!" said Dad. "You can't be serious?"

Spike had never felt more serious in his life. "Come on, Dad," he pleaded.

"Go on, Mr Enson," said Ebony. "Ali will love it."

"I'm not sure your mother will like it," said Dad, still looking at Spike in disbelief. "She will throw a complete wobbly! I just hope she likes the photos."

The Bonny Baby photographer was tall and skinny with a long, black pony-tail and a pinched expression on his face.

"That one's too big," he cried, jabbing a bony finger towards Spike. "Have you filled in your entry form?"

"It's just this one," said Dad as he wrestled Ali out of the carry-sling and leaned him against a pile of cushions.

A fancy digital camera was fixed into position on top of a tripod. The photographer squinted at the viewing screen.

Dad pranced about beside him and pulled funny faces to make Ali laugh. To Spike's surprise, it worked. Ali posed like a baby super-model.

The photographer zoomed in and out, clicking furiously. He loaded the photos on to his computer and examined the thumbnail images. He selected just five and printed out an A4 copy of each one. He spread them across the table and peered at them.

He scooped one up, snatched the

entry form out of Dad's hand, stapled the two sheets together and added them to a pile of others in a cardboard box.

He grabbed another photo and waved it under Dad's nose. "We enter the best picture in the contest," he said. "The second best is for the parent or carer. We take cash or credit cards."

"What about the others?" asked Spike as the photographer pushed the photo into a cheap-looking frame and Dad scrabbled in his wallet.

"Rejects," said the photographer, sweeping the remaining pictures off the table and into a bin.

"Rejects?" cried Spike. He sank to his knees to pick them up. "You must be joking! They can't be rejects – not of our Ali!"

That night, at home, Spike switched

on his bedside lamp and looked at the pictures again. For a Bonny Baby contest, they really were rejects. For proving that Ali Enson was an alien, though, they were perfect.

One of the pictures was over-exposed and Ali looked washed out and ghostly. In another, someone was walking past in the background and Ali had two heads. Spike held the third picture

up to the light and stared at it. This was the best one. Ali's skin had a faint green sheen and his eyes glowed like red-hot coals.

Forget the post, thought Spike suddenly, as he slipped out of bed and tucked the pictures into his rucksack. Forget school tomorrow, too. I will take the morning off and deliver the evidence to TJ in person. He hitched s pyjama bottoms and pulled his shoulders back to make himself feel braver. Getting hold of the pictures had been fairly easy. Now came the difficult bit.

Spike eased open his bedroom door and felt his way along the landing in the dark. Apart from the odd clank from the radiator pipes, the whole house was quiet, which wasn't surprising at two o'clock in the morning. Even Ali shut up occasionally!

Spike crept into the bathroom and stepped straight onto one of Ali's rubber bath toys. It squawked loudly and he froze.

Relax, he told himself. Mum's sleeping downstairs on the floor and Dad's exhausted. It will take more than a crushed duck to wake them.

All the same, he moved carefully. He clipped a clothes peg over his nose, pulled on a pair of pink rubber gloves and picked up the jam jar he had used to collect tadpoles last spring. Finally, he gulped a mouthful of air – and plunged his hand into the nappy bucket!

# Chapter 8

## UFONC

The UFO Notification Centre looked more impressive than Spike had expected. It was enormous – a gleaming skyscraper of steel and glass that soared up into the sky.

He stared at the reflections in the glass. At ground level, his own image gazed back at him from loads of different angles. Higher up, he could see the shopping centre and the bus station. Beyond that, the ring road and the canal twinkled in the sunlight.

Spike felt himself relax. The people inside probably dealt with alien invasions every day of their lives.

He walked up the steps to the entrance and pressed the buzzer. A closed circuit television camera whirred into action above his head and a woman's voice crackled over the intercom.

"Yes. Can I help you?"

"I have come to see TJ," said Spike. "I mean... er, Mr Hoppermann."

"Would that be Thomas J. Hoppermann of the UFO Notification Centre?"

"Yes," said Spike, relieved.

"Thought so," said the woman. "Happens all the time. This is Northborough Road. You need Northborough Passage. It's round the back."

"Thanks for your help," said Spike.

"You will need all the help you can get," muttered the woman as she snapped off the intercom.

70

I wonder what she means, thought Spike as he walked round to the back of the tower. It didn't take him long to work it out.

Northborough Passage was a scruffy little alley. It was where the drivers parked their trucks and vans when they made deliveries to the buildings on Northborough Road. It was where the people in the glass tower kept their dustbins.

Spike gazed at it in despair. There was nothing but piles of litter and a row of tatty lock-up garages.

He trudged up the alley and read the signs on the garage doors. Patel's Panel Beating and Re-Sprays, Bottled Gas Supplies, J. Bloggs, Scrap-Metal merchant... and then the one he almost wished wasn't there: Unidentified Flying Objects Notification Centre.

Spike sighed and banged on the door.

He was here now. What had he got to lose?

He heard a key being turned in the lock and the squeak of rusty hinges. Then the door swung out towards him.

He jumped backwards – partly to avoid being whacked in the face by the door and partly in surprise at his first glimpse of the man who must surely be TJ.

He looked more like an American wrestling champion than a scientist. Dad was pretty tall but TJ was at least half a metre taller and about three times as wide. His hair was shaved so close to his head that he looked bald and he was wearing black jeans and a tight T-shirt.

"Welcome to UFONC!" he bellowed. "Come in, kid. What can I do for you?"

Cautiously, Spike edged his way inside the lock-up and looked around.

It was dark and poky but he could just make out the shape of a telescope pointing out of the window. There were several other bits of equipment that he didn't recognize but most of them looked like they belonged to the scrap-metal merchant next door. Still, it was a start.

"I talked to you on the phone the other night," said Spike as he rooted through his rucksack. "I have brought the baby alien evidence."

"Way to go!" cried TJ. "The whispering Jensen kid. Didn't know whether I would hear from you again."

"Enson," said Spike, handing over the pictures and the jam jar. "Spike Enson."

TJ put the photographs inside a machine that looked like a prehistoric microwave. He flicked a switch and stared at them for a long time.

"The quality's not that great," he said, removing the ghost and two-headed pictures. "But they seem to be genuine."

Spike waited.

"He looks kinda like a regular kid,"

said TJ, examining the third picture more closely. "Except for those eyes – kinda cute and dangerously hypnotic all at the same time."

Not bad, thought Spike admiringly. It took me nearly six months to notice that.

TJ picked up the jam jar and looked at the poo sample. He unscrewed the lid and sniffed.

"Jeez!" he cried, slamming it shut. "Potent stuff!" He peered through the glass again. "Intriguing colour though."

"What do you reckon?" said Spike. "Do you think he's an alien?"

"It's kinda hard to say right off," said TJ. "I need to run the tests to be sure."

"Does it take long?" said Spike. "Could I stay and help?"

TJ roared with laughter. "Sure, kid.

Be my guest. As long as you have a couple of days to spare."

"Two days?" said Spike.

"Maybe more," said TJ as he guided Spike towards the door. "Take it easy, kid. As soon as I have something, I will give you a call."

# Chapter 9

## Shepherd's Pie

Once, before Larry Skinner had gone to work in the library, he had told Spike that bunking off school was dead easy.

What a doughnut, thought Spike as he scrambled up the back wall of the playground. Of course, it was easy. The hard part was getting back in!

He heaved himself to the top of the wall and looked around. The shock of what he saw sent him toppling over, head-first into a rhododendron bush.

A few metres away, hiding behind another bush, Mr Ford was having a crafty puff on his pipe.

Spike lifted his face out of the dirt and stared. Bang went any hope of being in time for lunch and band practice!

He clutched at his belly and prayed that Mr Ford would not hear it rumbling and spot him through the clouds of smoke. Somehow, he didn't and eventually, stiff with cramp and half-starved to death, Spike crawled out of his hiding place and slowly made his way to the classroom.

"Where were you this morning, Spike Enson?" asked Mr Ford, when he reached the E section on the register.

"Dentist, Sir," said Spike, doing his best to sound honest.

Mr Ford inspected the muddy stains on Spike's sweatshirt. "Really?" he said. "Have you brought your appointment card or a note from your parents?"

Spike lowered his gaze and said nothing. This was another little detail that Larry Skinner had forgotten to mention.

"Bring it tomorrow!" snapped Mr Ford. "I don't want to have to bother your parents about unauthorized absences. They have quite enough to deal with, looking after Ali."

"Yes, Sir," said Spike. "But not for much longer," he added, under his breath.

The first thing Spike noticed when he arrived home from school was how quiet it was. Not dead-of-night silent, just calm and peaceful, the way it had been before Ali arrived on the scene.

He stood in the hallway and listened. There was pan pipes music playing softly in the front room, and the sound of rain falling. For a second or two, he could not make sense of it. Then he remembered. It was one of Dad's relaxation CDs.

Spike poked his head round the door. Dad was sitting on his yoga mat in the lotus position, with his eyes closed.

Mum was sitting bolt upright in the armchair, supported by pillows. She was fast asleep but she had repainted her lips and nails and she was wearing a dress!

The carry-cot was empty. Where was Ali? Was it possible that he had already been teleported and was whizzing back to the Planet OsKarbi in a spaceship?

Fat chance, thought Spike. But he didn't care. Ali wasn't here. That was the important thing. He gave a silent cheer and tip-toed into the kitchen.

He was hungry but he didn't want to disturb Mum and Dad. They weren't to know that soon Ali would be gone for good and they would be able to relax any time they felt like it.

He helped himself to the bowl of shepherd's pie that was on the table and began to picture family life without Ali. He saw the three of them staying in a posh hotel at the seaside, him and Dad playing crazy-golf and swimming while Mum flung herself off the top of the cliffs to go hang-gliding.

Spike stuffed shepherd's pie into his mouth and let the vision spread out before him. It was like being the director of his own movie. He added sunshine and a few fluffy clouds, drifting in the breeze, then palm trees and surf.

He was just about to compose a drum solo for the sound track when Mum's voice rang out.

"Is that you, Spike?"

Spike shovelled up a last spoonful of mashed potato and went back to the front room.

"Are you feeling better now, Mum?"

"More or less," said Mum. "The doctor finally thinks it's OK for me to sit up again."

"As long as you take things easy," said Dad as he uncrossed his legs and stood up.

"That won't be hard if you and Mr Rivers have anything to do with it," said Mum. She looked at Spike and winked. "Was it you who told Mr Rivers I wasn't well? He came over

after the doctor left and said he would baby-sit Ali for an hour or so."

"He brought over a huge shepherd's pie too," said Dad. "Listen, son. Why don't you go and fetch Ali while I heat it up for dinner?"

"Dinner?" said Spike, glancing towards the kitchen.

Dad's eyes followed his gaze. "Good grief!" he cried. "Don't tell me you have eaten it. Not all of it!"

"Sorry," said Spike. "I was hungry."

Dad went bananas. He jumped up and down and tugged at his hair. Then he sent Spike to his room.

Spike fumed. How was he to know the pie was for their dinner? Why didn't Dad just phone for a take-away? Ali must be really getting to him. It was stress. You could not expect a human being to put up with an alien for six months without losing their temper once in a while.

# Chapter 10

## Ali Attack

Despite being sent to bed early the previous evening, Spike over-slept. Usually, his alien brother woke him up at the crack of dawn, bellowing for breakfast and a clean nappy. But today the house was quiet, just like yesterday afternoon.

Spike stared at his watch in disbelief. It was twenty-five past eight! If he didn't get a move on, Mr Ford would demand two notes from his parents – one to explain why he had been absent yesterday and one to explain why he was late today.

He scrambled out of bed and ran to the bathroom but the door was locked.

"Hurry up!" cried Spike, hammering on the door. "I'm going to be late."

"Hang on," called Dad. "I won't be a minute. Can you check on Ali for me?"

Spike sighed. The only explanation he had come up with for Ali's silence was that Dad had forgotten to pick him up from Mr Rivers the night before. But now he realized that Ali had kept quiet on purpose. He wanted to make Spike late. The horrible little sprog was actually trying to get him into trouble!

Spike went into Mum and Dad's room and looked down into the cot. Ali was sucking his toes and watching his spinning, musical, monkey mobile.

"Two more days," said Spike. "Then you are out of here." He paused. For the first time, it occurred to him that he had no idea what would happen to Ali once everyone knew he was an alien. "They will probably put you in the zoo," he went on. "Or do tests and experiments on you."

Spike shuddered and another new thought came to him. "Why can't you just be normal?" he said. "How are Mum and Dad going to feel when they realize you are an alien?"

Ali took his toes out of his mouth and smiled. It might have been wind because he followed it up with a burp. Then he scrunched up his face and began to howl.

"What are you doing?" cried Dad from the bathroom.

"Nothing!" called Spike, backing away from the cot. "I never touched him."

Ali gave another ear-splitting shriek and Spike leaped backwards in alarm. For a split-second, he flew through the air. Then he crashed down, straight into the baby-walker. His bottom was wedged tight and Spike felt the baby-walker whizz across the floor.

Then his head slammed into something very hard and solid and everything went black.

"Ouch!" said Spike when he woke up. "What time is it?"

Dad was sitting on the edge of his bed, holding his hand. "I'm not sure," he said, yawning. "About nine o'clock."

Spike struggled to sit up but his head felt like a lump of lead and he gave up instantly. "I'm late for school," he groaned.

"Take it easy," said Dad gently. "It will be a good few days before you are ready for school. You have been out cold for over twelve hours. It's nine in the evening. You are in hospital."

Spike opened his eyes again, wincing against the pain. This time he noticed the rows of beds stretching away on either side of him and the bright lights overhead.

Slowly, he remembered that Ali had attacked him! Well, not exactly attacked him, but it was definitely the baby alien's fault he had been hurt. Ali was dangerous. Mum and Dad had to be warned!

"Ali," he began. "It was Ali..."

"Shush," said Dad as he stroked Spike's forehead. "You need to rest. Don't worry about Ali. He's safe at home with Mum. They will come and visit you tomorrow."

Tomorrow, thought Spike drowsily. I will warn them tomorrow... and he drifted back to sleep.

Spike felt as if he had barely closed his eyes before he was woken up again by the crashing of bedpans and breakfast trolleys. But he knew it was morning. The overhead lights had been turned off and sunlight was streaming in through the gaps in the dirt on the windows.

A fierce-looking nurse shoved a cold stainless steel bowl under his still-tender bottom.

"Get a move on!" barked the nurse. "I can't wait all day."

Spike felt a flicker of sympathy for Ali. He had never realized what a luxury it was to be able to walk to the bathroom and not have people fiddling with your bits.

Breakfast was revolting. Sloppy scrambled eggs and mushy tinned tomatoes. Solid food is obviously a luxury too, thought Spike as he pushed away the tray and fought off the queasiness in his stomach.

Later, the doctor arrived with an army of medical students who peered at him over the top of their clip-boards.

"Bruised buttocks!" announced the doctor in a loud voice, before marching onto the next bed. "Oh yes," he added as an after-thought, "and severe concussion. We are keeping him in for observation."

Spike was miserable all day. Even at visiting time, he didn't get the chance to warn Mum and Dad about Ali because the Lovelace Twins turned up.

"Brought you a get-well card from Mr Ford and the rest of the class," said Ebony.

"What do you want to go crashing about in a baby-walker for?" said Kiera. "Honestly, Spike. You are weird."

# Chapter 11

## Bonny Baby

The next day, Mum came to see Spike again. This time she didn't bother to wait until visiting hours. It was still early morning. She ran down the ward, waving a newspaper out in front of her.

Spike was amazed. She was moving so fast it was hard to believe she had only just recovered from a bad back. She skidded to a halt at the end of his bed and glared at him.

"Spike Enson!" she cried. "What on earth have you been up to?"

For a second, Spike wondered if she had met Mr Ford in the supermarket again and found out about him skipping school. But it wasn't that, he could tell. It was something much

worse. Mum's eyes were red and her chin was trembling.

She slapped the newspaper down, sank into the armchair at the side of the bed and buried her face in her hands.

Spike began to feel scared. He could feel a lump at the back of his throat.

"Mum," he said, swallowing hard. "What is it?"

Mum's voice came out in a muffled whisper and he strained to hear what she was saying.

"Page four," she said. "Look at page four."

The newspaper was crumpled and torn, and Spike turned the pages anxiously until he found the right one.

"BONNY BABY!" proclaimed the headline in thick black print. Underneath, there was a picture of Ali – the one the photographer had chosen for the competition. Even

Spike could see that he was beautiful. Ali's eyes were almost twinkling and Spike could just make out the first of his baby teeth in the middle of his broad smile.

"Ali must have won!" cried Spike. "What's the matter? We thought you would be pleased."

"Pleased?" said Mum. "You know how I feel about competitions. For every winner, there are hundreds of losers. How could you talk Dad into entering Ali in a baby competition?"

"It's not my fault," said Spike desperately. "It was Kiera and Ebony's idea."

"Oh, Spike," muttered Mum. Her voice wobbled. "It's no good trying to blame the twins. Look at page five."

Spike shifted his gaze to the opposite page and saw that the headline continued.

"… OR ALIEN INVADER? YOU DECIDE!"

Underneath, there was a second picture – the one Spike had given to TJ as evidence!

Ali was tight-lipped and his eyes were hard and staring.

"Wow," said Spike, squinting at the newsprint. "This is wicked. Listen to this!"

His head was still aching but he braced himself and began to read aloud.

"The beautiful baby pictured above was awarded first prize in the Shoppers' Paradise Bonny Baby Competition. However, local professor, Thomas J. Hoppermann, formerly of the Ufology Department at the Metropolitan University, insists that tests on photographic evidence and stool samples prove that this particular bonny baby is not human."

Spike paused and glanced up at Mum before he read on.

"Late last night, a spokesman for the UFO Centre admitted that the credit for this amazing discovery should go to Spike Enson. Unfortunately, he could not be contacted at his home and was unavailable for comment."

Spike put down the paper.

"I was right," he said. "TJ has analysed his poo and everything. It's true, Mum. Ali *is* an alien!"

"You don't understand," sniffed Mum. "I'm upset because of you, not Ali."

It's shock, thought Spike. She's suffering from shock and she's confused.

"They should have called him a nutty professor, not a local professor," said Mum. Her voice was gradually getting louder again. "He should be locked up, along with the foolish people who agreed to print this nonsense."

Spike noticed that some of the other patients and a couple of the nurses were watching them. But as soon as they saw him looking, they began examining their fingernails or gazing up at the cracks in the ceiling.

"Mum," he whispered. "I'm sorry. Are you OK?"

Suddenly Spike felt himself being swept up into Mum's arms and squeezed. He spat out a stray mouthful of her headscarf and sighed with relief. If he had to choose between being scared to death or squeezed to death, he would definitely go for the squeeze.

The last time she had held him this tight, remembered Spike, she was the one who had been in hospital. It was exactly six months ago – right after she had given birth to Ali. She had bawled her eyes out but afterwards she laughed and told him she was as happy as a pig in muck.

Spike looked up at her now and waited for the smile of happiness to spread across her face. But it didn't come. Her face was grim and she scowled at the patient in the next bed until he looked away.

"We need to talk," said Mum. "But

we can't do it here. The entrance is crawling with crowds of crazy reporters, all wanting an interview or a picture of you. We will have to sneak out the back way. You get dressed while I call a taxi."

# Chapter 12

## The Talk

On the way home, Spike leaned against Mum's shoulder and dozed. It was the only way to avoid thinking about whatever it was that Mum wanted to talk about.

He opened his eyes just as the taxi pulled up in front of the house. There was a small crowd of people gathered on the pavement outside.

Mum saw them too. "Drive on!" she yelled at the top of her voice.

The driver leaped up from his seat in shock. He landed back down with a thud and his foot rammed the accelerator. The taxi shot off along the road, leaving a trail of burning rubber.

"Sorry," said Mum over the sound of screeching tyres. "Can you drop us off at a phone box? I have forgotten my mobile."

"Listen, lady," said the driver. "If you are on the run, leave me out of it." He swerved round the next corner and slammed on the brakes. "Go on," he said. "Hop it!"

"How much do I owe you?" said Mum.

"Forget it!" said the driver. He was beginning to panic. "Out! Get out!"

"Come on," said Mum, climbing out and tugging at Spike's sleeve. "I think there's a pay-phone in the launderette."

She charged across the road towards the shops and Spike limped after her.

It was hot inside the launderette and there was a strong smell of detergent and bleach. Spike flopped onto a bench and leaned his aching head against a basket of cool, damp sheets.

Mum was already speaking into the phone but she wasn't talking to Dad.

"Mr Rivers? Is that you? Mrs Enson here. You have to help us. There's a bunch of paparazzi camped outside our house. We need about five minutes. Can you keep them busy? Offer them a cup of tea or an exclusive interview or something..." She paused, looking anxious. "Thanks, Mr Rivers. You are an angel!"

A few minutes later, Spike and Mum slipped into the house completely unnoticed.

Good one, thought Spike, as he glanced across the road. Mr Rivers had the reporters backed up against the privet chickens and he was making threatening gestures with his electric hedge-trimmer.

Inside, Dad was pacing up and down the front room, clutching Ali against his chest.

Spike stared at him. The frown lines on Dad's forehead criss-crossed like a BMX track and all the colour seemed to have drained away from his face. Instead of warm, chocolate-brown, his skin was a yucky greyish-green.

Mum told Spike to sit on the sofa. He felt as if he had been led to the wall in front of a firing squad. He took a deep breath and waited for the first bullet.

"Son," said Dad quietly, echoing Mum's earlier words. "We need to talk."

Spike looked up at them both. In a round-about way, he had just told them that their beloved baby son was an alien. Of course they needed to talk.

"It's about your adoption," said Mum.

Spike's heart did a back-flip and he felt his brain scramble. Somehow, Mum and Dad were missing the point. They

had told him he was adopted years ago. Why did they want to talk about that now?

"We know it's been hard on you since Ali was born," said Mum. "But until now I don't think we realized how much."

"We just wish you had come to us," said Dad. "Instead of running off to Mr Hoppermann and the newspapers with all this talk about aliens."

"You are our son," said Mum, taking his hand. "Being adopted doesn't make you an outsider. We love you just as much as we love Ali."

Spike stared at them, shocked. He must be dreaming. This was a nightmare – some horrible side-effect from the bang on the head that the doctors hadn't noticed.

Mum and Dad thought *he* was the outsider. They thought *he* was the alien!

"No, no. You... you have g...got it wrong," stammered Spike. "It's not me. It's Ali! Ali is the alien."

"We know, love," said Mum gently. "You are right. Ali *is* an alien... but then... so are we!"

Spike snatched his hand away but Dad crouched down in front of him and looked into his eyes.

"Me and your mother came in peace from the planet Aledela IV. We adopted you so we could fit in with life on Earth while we carried out our assignment. Ali is our natural son."

Spike felt a shiver run down his spine. He opened and closed his mouth several times but no sound came out. They were joking. They had to be.

"Special Project for the Investigation of Children on Earth," said Mum.

"That's why we called you Spike."

"We had to swap Children for Kids, of course," went on Dad. "Otherwise, we would have had to call you Spice."

Spike felt the hot sting of tears in his eyes. He heard the blood pounding in his head. But he still could not speak.

"You have blown our cover," said Dad. "Now every news agency on Earth wants Ali's story but there's only one way the story can end. Everyone from every branch of science will be chasing after him. They will want to run tests. There will be needles, samples, biopsies and probably much worse."

"We have to leave," said Mum. "Now."

"A ship's on the way from Aledela as we speak," said Dad.

He glanced at his watch. "We have

about forty-seven minutes to get ready and then we..."

Ali began to scream. He screamed so loudly that he drowned out the rest of Dad's words. But it didn't matter. Spike wasn't listening any more. Inside, he was screaming too.

# Chapter 13

## Jump!

Spike fled through the back door to the garden shed and locked himself inside. He hauled his drum-kit out from behind the lawn mower and flung himself down on the stool.

Stuff them, he thought. I wish I had never been adopted. I wish I had never set eyes on any of them!

He slammed his foot down on the bass pedal and the sound boomed out, rattling the walls. He clenched his fists around the drumsticks and crashed them against the cymbals until he blocked out the sound of Mum knocking on the door and begging to be let in.

"Go away!" yelled Spike as he laid into the tom-tom and snare drums. "Get lost! Leave me alone!"

He hammered and banged, blasting his ear-drums with the thunderous noise. Inside, his blood raced and his heart pounded with the same furious rhythm. But he played on and on. Faster and faster. Louder and louder.

It was dark when Spike unlocked the shed and crept back into the house. None of the lights had been switched on and there was a deathly hush about the place.

For a few moments, Spike stood in the kitchen, alone and uncertain.

Then he yelled at the top of his voice. "Mum! Dad! Where are you?"

There was no reply.

"Ali!" he bellowed, even louder, but still no one answered.

Spike went into the front room and stood shivering in the silence. Through the window he could just make out the chickens in Mr Rivers' hedge against the moonlit sky. But the reporters were gone. The street was deserted, like the house.

Spike shuddered. There was a lump the size of the dwarf planet Pluto in his throat and his heart felt heavier than a neutron star. All his anger and rage had died with the last fading drum-beat.

That's it, he thought miserably. I told them to go away and they have. They have taken Ali and they have gone. They didn't even say goodbye.

Spike slumped against the window and pressed his face against the coolness of the glass. He stared up at the stars, twinkling in the blue-black sky. Which tiny dot of light was Aledela IV? Sadly, he realized he would never know.

He whispered into the darkness. "Goodbye, Dad. Bye, Mum. Bye, Ali."

A sudden rustling sound shattered the silence and made him jump. He turned and peered anxiously around the darkened room.

More mad scientists, he thought, looking for Ali. Or the paparazzi... looking for me? But, no! There it was again. It was coming from somewhere near the empty carry-cot.

Spike stumbled across the room, tripping over baby toys. He flicked on the light and looked down at the pile of blankets in the cot. It moved!

Spike gasped. His heart missed a beat... and then a tiny brown fist shot into the air from under the blanket and Spike's chest flooded with the same mixture of feelings he remembered from the park. Brotherly love – and huge relief.

"Ali!" cried Spike as he lifted him out. "I thought you were gone."

He held his baby brother against his heart and hugged him tight. Spike smiled and Ali beamed back at him. Then Spike heard the familiar gurgling sound from Ali's other end as he filled his nappy.

"Oh, yuck!" said Spike automatically. But he checked himself. "It's OK, Ali. I will change you."

He carried Ali upstairs and set him down on the changing table in Mum and Dad's room.

"You stink!" said Spike as he peeled off the nappy. "But I suppose I will have to get used to it. I think Mum and Dad have gone. They have left us both."

Ali kicked his legs and gave a little whimper.

"It's OK," said Spike as he set to

work with the baby wipes and talcum powder. "I will look after you. You are my brother, Ali. I don't care if you are an alien."

He stuck down the tabs on the nappy and bundled Ali up into his arms.

"Good work, son," boomed Dad's voice behind him.

Spike spun round. "I thought you had gone!"

"No way," said Dad. "Not without you two. You should know by now that we would never leave either of you kids behind!"

"I have been packing essentials for the trip. You know the sort of thing: nappies, drum-sticks, headphones... Your mother's re-calibrating the particle accelerator."

"What?" said Spike.

"On the starship. She's waiting," said Dad. He took Ali from Spike's arms. "It's up on the roof. Come on. We have to get going."

Dad turned and left the bedroom and Spike heard him climbing the folding metal step-ladder into the attic.

Spike looked around the room and caught a glimpse of himself in Mum's dressing table mirror. Now even his own brown skin seemed to be tinged with green. There was a glint in his eye and a mischievous smile on his lips.

There was also a wicked idea in his head and he could not resist it. He picked up the phone and punched in the number for the Lovelace Twins.

"Just wanted to let you know," he told the answering machine. "My mum and dad would not let you look after

Ali if you were the last baby-sitters on Earth. It's too far from the Planet Aledela!"

Spike climbed into the attic and then through the sky-light onto the roof.

He stared. The starship, a gleaming silver hulk which seemed to fill the sky and stretch to the horizon, was humming and hovering a few metres away from the chimney.

TJ's phones must be ringing off the hook, thought Spike. Half the town must be able to hear it. The whole town must be able to see it.

Mum's face appeared at the airlock compartment hatch. "Spike," she called gently. "Jump!"

It's now or never, thought Spike. He had to choose. He could jump back down into the attic and become an orphan Earthling again – or he could jump onto the starship with his family and fly off to a new life as an adopted alien son on the Planet Aledela.

Spike jumped.

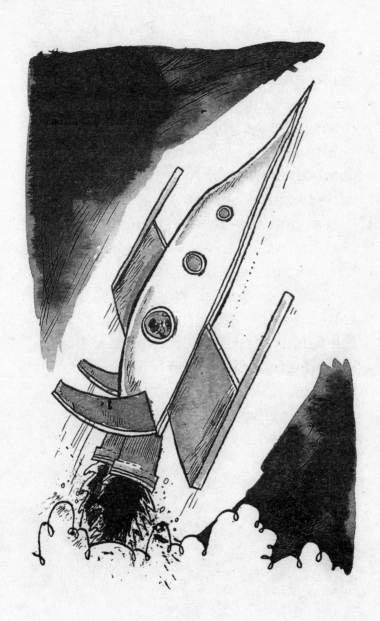

# About the author

Malaika Rose Stanley grew up in Birmingham
in the UK. She has worked as a teacher in
Zambia, Uganda, Germany, Switzerland and
Britain. She is now a full-time writer. She runs
creativity and writing workshops for children and
adults. Her books include *Man Hunt, Operation X*
and *Dad Alert* and she also writes short stories.

Malaika enjoys travel, yoga, watching football,
jazz singing, reading and gardening. She lives
with her family in north London.

# About the illustrator

Sarah was born one snowy November day
in sub-zero Derbyshire, UK. She graduated
from Falmouth College of Arts in 2001
and Kingston University in 2004.

Sarah loves colour, line, characters, humour,
detail, nature, irony and many cups of tea.
She also paints and writes.

Sarah lives in London and works from
Happiness At Work Studios in sunny Wapping.

# Also available from Tamarind Books

Jamie MacDoran is a pretty cool teen.
He's a basketball ace and a skateboarding
fanatic. He's even popular with the girls.
But when his dad dies suddenly
in a car accident everything changes.
He and his mother are forced to fly from
America to a small Scottish island to bury him.
There, in the run-down family castle Jamie
soon hears talk of an ancient inheritance.
He's more than just an average skater boy.
But how far is he willing to go to prove it?

By Emmy and BAFTA nominated
screenwriter Ken Howard

ISBN 9781848530331

Ferris Fleet: the Wheelchair Wizard
*by Annie Dalton*
*Illustrated by Carl Pearce*

Oscar's mum moves the family to World Nine
hoping for a quiet life. But it's not to be... Mum is
soon called back to her very important job with the
Cosmic Peace Police, and needs to find a babysitter
for Oscar and baby Ruby. They choose Ferris Fleet,
the coolest, funkiest young magician ever seen,
and his magical wheelchair, Wonderwheels.
It's just as well, because all is not as safe as it
seems in their new neighbourhood...

New title in the series coming in 2011
Selected for the Summer Reading Challenge
Listed in National Literacy Trust Recommended Reads

ISBN 978 1 870 51673 0

Hurricane
*by Verna Wilkins*
*Illustrated by Tim Clarey*

Troy and Nina are sent home early from
school because of a hurricane warning. Instead
of going straight home, they make the mistake
of stopping to visit a friend. The storm breaks,
and the children get caught up in the terrible
winds. This exciting adventure brings to life the
atmosphere of a hurricane on a small tropical
island and its devastating effects.

ISBN 978 1 870 51676 1

The Day Ravi Smiled
*by Gillian Lobel*
*Illustrated by Kim Harley*

Joy loves riding horses at Penniwells Riding
Centre. All her friends do too. But there's a boy
there called Ravi who doesn't talk, is very shy
and never looks happy. Joy worries about him.

She doesn't know he's autistic.

One day, she needs Ravi's help...

ISBN 978 1 870 51676 1

Ben's Birthdays
*by Elizabeth Hawkins*
*Illustrated by Paul Cemmick*

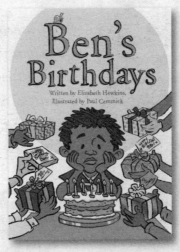

Everyone has had more birthdays than Ben.
His sister Jessica has had 10. Dad has had 38!
But Ben's birthday never seems to come.
When Ben stumbles across a talking snail
who grants him a wish, Ben has the
chance to change all that...

ISBN 978 1 848 53018 8

# Tamarind biography series

*"The inspirational story of a inspirational man, very well written, presented in a really accessible manner and a real joy to read."*
Malorie Blackman

Also available
Michelle Obama

# Biographies of black British icons for 9+ years

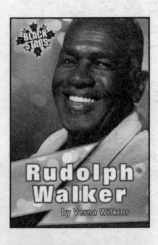